Thank you for purchasing this book!

I wanted to show my appreciation that you support my work so I've put together a free gift for you.

elliewoods.info/owlet

Just visit the link above to download printable coloring pages of the characters.

Disclaimer and Terms of Use:

Effort has been made to ensure that the information in this book is accurate and complete, however, the author and the publisher do not warrant the accuracy of the information, text and graphics contained within the book due to the rapidly changing nature of science, research, known and unknown facts and internet. The Author and the publisher do not hold any responsibility for errors, omissions or contrary interpretation of the subject matter herein. This book is presented solely for motivational and informational purposes only.

SAY PLEASE,
Little Owlet

by **ELLIE J. WOODS**

illustrated by
MIRRA OBLAKOVA

The little Owlet lived in a cozy tree house
With his fluffy owl family and a pet mouse.
His Mom would cook some healthy food,
Making it delicious for her hungry brood.

Dad watched "The Birds' News" on TV,
Holding a newspaper and sipping tea.

Granny Owl knitted scarves and socks
For the baby owls not to catch cold.
His sister Lily was fond of delicate wild flowers
Which she liked to carefully paint for hours.

The Owlet's cheerfulness had no end
And the pet mouse was his best friend.
They played under the table and on the couch
With Daddy's striped ties and Mommy's pouch.

The mouse would hide behind the flower pot,
The Owlet would quickly find him and laugh a lot.
They had so much fun, so much pleasure,
That every day seemed to be a real treasure.

The only thing that was not quite right -
The Owlet was a bit rude and impolite,
His Mom and Dad were not very glad,
They wanted him to be a well-bred little lad.

He used to shout:

"Give me this!" and "Give me that!"

"I want milk chocolate,

I don't want the nasty raw salad!"

His Mommy was very patient indeed,
She calmed him down with a gentle plead:
"My dear, sweet honey, you must behave nice,
You should say 'please' at least once, maybe twice!
Every time use the magic word
And be a nice, well-mannered bird."

One day the Owlet and his friend mouse
Were running around their cozy house.
They were playing the game of hide-and-seek,
Yelling out loud when one would peek.

The mouse rushed into the clean, bright kitchen
The Owlet chased after, trying to catch him.
Mommy Owl was baking a fruit cake
With cherries, cream and coconut flakes.

The little Owlet smelled it soon
And started rattling with a spoon:
"I want the cake, I want it now!
I don't care why, I don't care how!
I want it here, on my lovely plate!
It must be yummy; it must be great!"

Mommy felt terribly sad and upset
With the graceless words the little Owlet said.
"If you'd like to get the delicious cake,

Don't be rude, don't make a mistake,
Always use the simple magic rule,
The word 'Please' is such an easy tool."

"Dear Mommy, please, please, please,
Let me sit on your soft knees
And have the yummy cherry cake -
It looks so pretty – I just can't wait!"

"There you go, my little one,
Now you are my lovely son,
Being well-mannered and polite,
You bring so much joy and delight."

She kissed the Owlet and held him tight
And gave him a piece of cake: red and white.

All the family were as happy as they could be,
Enjoying the fruit cake and chamomile tea;

Proud of the little Owlet, who had learnt the word
And became a well-mannered, polite little bird.

Thank you for purchasing this book!

I wanted to show my appreciation that you support my work so I've put together a free gift for you.

elliewoods.info/owlet

Just visit the link above to download printable coloring pages of the characters.

A personal note from the author

If you enjoyed this book, please leave a favorable review at the book's Amazon page. Reviews will help others to make an informed decision before buying my book and are a great encouragement.

Thank you so much!

Yours,

Ellie J. Woods.

49346250R00018

Made in the USA
San Bernardino, CA
21 May 2017